THUNDERBIRDS

THE PERILS OF PENELOPE

BY AISLING O'HAGAN

B☘XTREE

THE PERILS OF PENELOPE

It was late afternoon when Lady Penelope had a call from her old friend, the scientist Sir Jeremy Hodge. But within the hour she had set off from her large stately home in her gadget-filled FAB 1 Rolls, driven by her trusty chauffeur, Parker. Late that same evening, Lady Penelope was seated at a table with her friend, on a terrace outside a café in Paris.

'Now, Sir Jeremy,' said Penelope, after they'd talked for a while. 'You didn't bring me all this way for nothing. Why the air of mystery?'

'What I'm going to tell you is absolutely top-secret,' whispered Sir Jeremy. 'You remember my old friend, Professor Borinder?'

'You mean your colleague at the Inter-Research Laboratory?'

'Absolutely,' said Sir Jeremy. 'Two nights ago, after the International Science Conference here in Paris, I saw him off by train to Anderbad. But when the train got there, he wasn't on it.'

But before Penelope had time to find out more, a shot rang out and a bullet shattered the glass in her hand...

'Pardon me, M'Lady,' Parker was closing down the loaded headlamps of the Rolls parked nearby. 'But the drink was drugged.'

Suddenly a stranger who had been sitting two tables away, made a dash for the door.

'Look,' said Penelope. 'He dropped these matches and there's a crest on the cover.'

'Hmm,' said Sir Jeremy. 'May I suggest a visit to the heraldic archives in the morning to look it up?'

'Good idea. And now you'd better tell me what this is all about.'

Travelling back to the city, Sir Jeremy explained to Penelope that he and Borinder had recently discovered a highly top-secret method of turning sea water into fuel. If the operation wasn't performed correctly, though, it could contaminate the waters of the world.

'So if the formula gets into the wrong hands the results could be pretty terrifying,' said Penelope. 'What would you like us to do?'

'You must help me find Professor Borinder.'

'We will have to work fast. These men will stop at nothing.'

Later that night, at International Rescue's top secret headquarters, Jeff Tracy received an urgent signal from Lady Penelope.

'So you see how serious the situation is, Jeff,' said Penelope after she'd explained.

'Yes I do. Think you'll need any help?'

'I think we might,' replied Penelope. 'Sir Jeremy and I are taking the night train to Anderbad to make some investigations.'

'OK, Penny. I'll send the boys in Thunderbird 2 and all the equipment we think you'll need. They'll meet you at Anderbad.'

Once again the forces of International Rescue were called on a life-saving mission. Before Penelope could close her powder case receiver, Virgil, Gordon and Alan were propelled into the cockpit of Thunderbird 2. From here they set in motion the conveyor belt that carried the six huge, green rescue pods underneath its wings.

'Good luck boys,' shouted their father as the engines roared. 'Keep in touch at all times'.

The next day, as planned, Penelope met Sir Jeremy at the heraldic Library to see whether the matchbook might give them any more clues to the kidnapping.

Once inside, it became even more clear that someone was trying to dispose of them. A grey-haired librarian showed them to a vault at the bottom of a rickety staircase. But they hardly had time to blow the dust from the files when the door was slammed shut.

'Hey, what's going on?' shouted Sir Jeremy.

'I think I can guess,' said Penelope. 'I smell gas. And not a window in the place.'

I knew that sinister-looking librarian was a phoney,' said Sir Jeremy. 'What are we going to do now?'

Luckily for them, Parker was keeping watch outside. The second he received the distress call from Penelope he turned the Rolls round, lifted the back flaps and fired two grappling hooks through the library and into the vault door. Pressing his foot hard on the excelerator, he tore the door from its hinges.

'Just in time,' gasped Sir Jeremy. 'Are you OK, Penelope?'

'Perfectly. I knew Parker wouldn't let us down. Next step is to get to Anderbad. Come on, Sir Jeremy. You and I have a train to catch.'

That night, as Penelope and Sir Jeremy boarded the express for

Anderbad, Jeff Tracy was carefully working out another rescue plan for the Thunderbird team.

'And when you get to Anderbad, boys, land on hill GF Mark 2. From there you should get a good view of Penelope's train as it comes out of the tunnel. Parker will follow by car and head for the station.'

'OK, Father,' said Virgil from the controls of Thunderbird 2. 'Leave it to us.'

Once they were settled in their train compartments, Sir Jeremy and Penelope set about asking some questions. They started with the attendant who would have looked after the missing professor on his fateful journey. But the man assured them that no such person had boarded the train.

'Well, perhaps I imagined the whole thing,' said Sir Jeremy gloomily.

'Nonsense,' said Penelope, trying to reassure him. 'That man is clearly hiding something. Let's forget the whole thing for a while, order dinner and get a good night's sleep.'

As they made their way to the dining carriage, little did the couple know that their attendant was being interrogated again. This time by the same sinister-looking rogue who had turned up at the library,

and at the café two nights before.

'But I told you,' pleaded the attendant, 'I told them nothing!'

'Just do as I tell you,' snapped the crook, 'or you will regret it. I am setting a little trap that not even Lady Penelope can escape from.'

As the express train hurtled through mountainous terrain, Penelope and Sir Jeremy became more convinced that Professor Borinder had met his kidnappers on the same journey.

After reporting back to Jeff Tracy at International Rescue Headquarters, the two decided to get an early night to prepare them for the day ahead.

It wasn't long before Penelope was woken by noises outside her room. Quietly taking a gun from her purse, she opened her door, but only saw a grey haired attendant disappearing into the next carriage.

'Someone's been listening at my door,' she explained to Sir Jeremy, after waking him. 'Come with me, but be careful not to disturb the other passengers.'

They'd nearly searched all of the train when Penelope spotted the attendant going through her bags in the luggage racks. At gun point

she demanded an explanation.

'Oh..er, I am your new attendant,' explained the startled man. 'I was merely trying to work out which passengers were leaving the train at Anderbad. Now if there are no more questions I will bid you goodnight.'

After he left Penelope and Sir Jeremy realised their new attendant was the villain who tried to dispose of them in Paris. It was exactly one hour after dawn when Thunderbird 2 touched down on the hill that Jeff Tracy had mapped out for them.

'Hey, Father was right,' shouted Gordon, looking down over the vast mountains. 'We've got a great view of the tracks.'

'Yeah,' agreed Alan. 'And look, there's the end of the Anderbad tunnel.'

Moments later, Parker arrived in the pink Rolls, and was sent on by Virgil to meet the train at Anderbad station.

After a restless night, Penelope and Sir Jeremy had risen early to prepare for their arrival, and to follow the movements of their phoney attendant. But, halfway through breakfast, the train sped into the Anderbad tunnel and came to a sudden halt.

'There must have been a power failure!' exclaimed Penelope.

'You're right, Lady Penelope,' said a voice in the darkness. 'There has indeed been a power failure. Now come with me, please...'

Back up the hill, the boys were beginning to get impatient when Parker called through from the station with some worrying news. Penelope's train had broken down in the tunnel, and had just arrived at the station without her or Sir Jeremy on board. Virgil sensed danger and immediately called base.

'Does Parker know where the breakdown took place?' asked Jeff.

'Seventeen miles from Anderbad,' replied Virgil.

'Right boys,' said their father. 'You'd better get on the monotruck and go find them.'

Wasting no time, Virgil opened up one of the pods carried by Thunderbird 2. At the press of a button a giant armoured truck emerged from inside, heaving itself forward on wide caterpillar tracks.

While Alan stayed behind to keep contact with base, Virgil and

Gordon set off on the 17-mile journey into the heart of the Anderbad tunnel. Even International Rescue could not have realised the terrible danger Lady Penelope and Sir Jeremy were in. Bound and gagged, the couple had been taken to a subterranean lair, deep in the tunnel. From here the master of disguises had taken control of the entire rail network.

'I suppose this is how you kidnapped Professor Borinder,' said Sir Jeremy.

'That is correct,' replied the imposter. And he opened a side door to reveal Sir Jeremy's old friend.

'Professor Borinder!' exclaimed Sir Jeremy. 'Thank heaven you're safe. Who is this scoundrel?'

'Forgive me,' interrupted their captor. 'I am Doctor Godber. You, no doubt, have never heard of me but I know all about you and that fascinating discovery you made, and I intend to make use of it.'

'You will never get us to reveal the formula,' shouted Professor Borinder. 'Never!'

'Oh I think I will,' said the villain. And, raising the blind from the window the two men were stunned to see Lady Penelope suspended

on a ladder above the track. 'Now all we have to do is wait for the next train to pass through. It should be about 9 minutes.'

'You barbaric fiend,' yelled Sir Jeremy. 'Cut the power. You must stop that train!' Less than a mile away, Virgil and Gordon were desperately searching the darkness for clues that would lead to their missing friends.

'We've come over 16 miles, Virgil,' said Gordon. 'They must be around here somewhere. Let's see what's around that corner.'

As the mighty truck heaved itself round the last bend in the tunnel, Virgil suddenly slammed his foot on the break, bringing it to a screeching halt. Ahead, in the darkness, they could just see Lady Penelope lying in the path of the oncoming train.

They had to act quickly! Grabbing their weapons, the two boys crawled along the track until they heard voices nearby. With seconds to spare, Gordon threw himself into the room where the two men were held and wrestled with the villain, forcing him to drop his gun.

Meanwhile, when he knew it was safe to act, Virgil took aim and fired, breaking the rope that bound Penelope in the path of the express train. Seconds later the mighty engine roared past and the two rolled together under the track to safety. No one was more

relieved to see the bright red monotruck emerge from the tunnel than Alan and Parker, who had been waiting anxiously at the top of the hill with Thunderbird 2. Excitedly they called base and reassured Jeff Tracy that another rescue operation was successfully completed.

'That's great boys,' said their father. 'Now all we have to do is hand over that villain Godber to the authorities and make sure he never tries it again.'

'Leave it to us, Mr Tracy,' said Parker. 'That rotten scoundrel won't be trying anything for a while.'

When the team eventually arrived back in Paris, clean and refreshed, they decided to treat themselves to a celebration night out at an exclusive restaurant. Jeff Tracy was so pleased at his sons' work he even flew Tin-Tin over to keep Alan company.

'Why, you haven't touched your drink, Penelope old girl,' said Sir Jeremy, as the evening drew to a close. 'Perhaps the day's events have been a bit too much for you.'

'Far from it, Sir Jeremy,' replied Penelope. 'It's just that I remember the last time I ordered a drink in Paris I was shot at by a man in a pink Rolls Royce...'

First published in the UK 1992 by BOXTREE LIMITED,
36 Tavistock Street, London WC2E 7PB

1 3 5 7 9 10 8 6 4 2

Copyright (c) 1992 ITC Entertainment Group Ltd.
Licensed by Copyright Promotions Ltd.

Design by Root Associates Ltd.

1-85283-716-0

Printed in Great Britain by Butler & Tanner Ltd.

A catalogue record for this book is available from the British Library.